HORRID HENRY'S
Nightmare

HORRID HENRY'S
Nightmare

Francesca Simon
Illustrated by Tony Ross

Orion
Children's Books

Horrid Henry's Nightmare was originally published in *Horrid Henry's Nightmare*, but appears here for the first time in a single volume with brand-new full-colour illustrations.

ORION CHILDREN'S BOOKS

Horrid Henry's Nightmare first appeared in *Horrid Henry's Nightmare*
First published in Great Britain in 2013 by Orion Children's Books
This Early Reader edition first published in Great Britain in 2019 by Hodder
and Stoughton

1 3 5 7 9 10 8 6 4 2

Text © Francesca Simon, 2013
Illustrations © Tony Ross, 2013

ISBN 978 1 51010 626 0

Printed and bound in China

The paper and board used in this book are from well-managed forests and other
responsible sources.

Orion Children's Books
An imprint of
Hachette Children's Group
Part of Hodder & Stoughton
Carmelite House
50 Victoria Embankment
London EC4Y 0DZ

An Hachette UK Company
www.hachette.co.uk
www.hachettechildrens.co.uk
www.horridhenry.co.uk

For the wonderful Tim Sheader

Look out for:

Don't Be Horrid, Henry!
Horrid Henry's Birthday Party
Horrid Henry's Holiday
Horrid Henry's Underpants
Horrid Henry Gets Rich Quick
Horrid Henry and the Football Fiend
Horrid Henry's Nits
Horrid Henry and Moody Margaret
Horrid Henry's Thank You Letter
Horrid Henry and the School Fair
Horrid Henry and the Zombie Vampire
Horrid Henry's Hike

There are many more
Early Reader titles available.

For a complete list visit
horridhenry.co.uk

Contents

Chapter 1

". . . and then the slime-covered,
flesh-eating zombie, fangs dripping
blood, lurched into school, wailing
and gnashing and — pouncing!"
screamed Rude Ralph,
grabbing Horrid Henry.
Henry shrieked.
"Ha ha, gotcha," said Ralph.

Horrid Henry's heart pounded. How he loved being scared! What could be better than having a sleepover with Ralph, and both of them trying to scare the other?

He reached into the Purple Hand Fort's top secret skull and bones biscuit tin, and scoffed a big handful of chocolate gooey chewies. Scary stories and chocolate. Whoopie!

"Watch out, Ralph," said Henry. "I'm gonna tell you about the alien acid monster who creeps—"

"Smelly toads," piped a little voice outside the Purple Hand Fort. Grrr.

"Hide," hissed Horrid Henry.
Rude Ralph belched.

"I know you're in there, Henry,"
said Peter.
"No I'm not," said Henry.
"And I said the password, so you have
to let me in," said Peter. "It's my fort
too. Mum said so."

Horrid Henry sighed loudly. Why
on earth, of all the possible brothers
in the world, did he have to get
stuck with Peter? Why oh why,
when younger brothers were being
distributed, did he get landed with a
tell-tale, smelly nappy baby?

"All right, come in," said Henry.
Perfect Peter crept through
the branches.
"Why is it so dark in here?"
said Peter.

"None of your business, baby,"
said Henry. "You've been in,
now get out."
"Yeah, wriggle off, worm,"
said Ralph.

Chapter 2

"No babies allowed in the Purple
Hand Fort," said Henry.
Perfect Peter stuck out his lower
lip. "I'm going to tell Mum you
wouldn't let me stay in the fort. And
that you called me a baby."
"Go ahead, baby boo boo,"
said Henry.

"MUM!" screamed Peter. "Henry called me baby boo boo."

"Stop being horrid, Henry, and be
nice to your brother," shouted Mum.
"Or I'll send Ralph home."

"I wasn't being horrid," bellowed Henry. Oh to be a wizard and turn Peter into a toadstool.

"Okay, Peter, you can stay," snarled
Henry. "But you'll be sorry."
"No I won't," said Peter.
"We're telling scary stories,"
said Ralph.
"And you hate scary stories,"
said Henry.

Peter considered. It was true, he hated being scared. And almost everything scared him. But maybe that was last week. Maybe now that he was a week older he wouldn't be scared any more.

"I'm brave now," said Peter.

Horrid Henry shrugged. "Well, just don't blame me when you wake up screaming tonight," he shrieked.

Peter jumped. Should he stay and listen to these terrible tales? Then he squared his shoulders. He wasn't a baby, whatever Henry said. He was a big boy.

Horrid Henry told his scariest story about the child-eating vampire werewolf. Rude Ralph told his scariest story about the wailing graveyard ghost who slurped up babies. Then Henry told his most scary story ever in the history of the world: the alien acid monster and zombie mummy who—

"I know a scary story,"
interrupted Peter.
"We don't want to hear it,"
said Henry.
"It's really scary, I promise," said
Peter. "Once upon a time there
was a bunny . . ."

"SCARY stories!" shouted
Rude Ralph.
"Once upon a time there was a really
big bunny," said Peter. "And one day
his little tail fell off."
Peter paused.

"Is that it?" said Henry.
"Yes," said Peter.
"Blecccccchhhh," belched
Rude Ralph.
"That's your idea of a scary story?"
said Henry. "A bunny with no tail?"

"Wouldn't you be scared if you
were a bunny and your tail fell off?"
said Peter.

"Isn't it time for you to practise your cello?" said Henry.
Peter gasped.
He didn't ever like to miss a day's practice.

Perfect Peter trotted off.
Phew. Worm-free at last.

"Now, as I was telling you, Ralph,"
said Horrid Henry, "there was once a
zombie mummy that roamed . . ."

Chapter 3

NO!!!!!
Horrid Henry lay in bed in his dark bedroom, trembling. What a horrible, horrible nightmare. All about a ghost bunny with huge teeth and no tail, charging at him waving a gigantic needle. Ugggh. His heart was pounding so fast he thought it would pop out of his chest.

But what to do, what to do?
Henry was too scared to stay in bed.
Henry was too scared to move. Don't
be an idiot, snarled Devil 1. There is
no such thing as a ghost bunny. Yeah,
you lummox, snarled Devil 2.

What a wimp.
Frankly, I'm disappointed.
But Horrid Henry was too terrified
to listen to reason. What if that alien
acid monster or the ghost bunny was
hiding under his bed?

Horrid Henry wanted to lean over and check, but he couldn't. Because what if the wailing graveyard ghost had sneaked into his wardrobe and was just waiting to GRAB him?

Worst of all, there was Ralph, snoring
happily away in his sleeping bag.
How could he just lie there when he
was going to get gobbled up
any second?

"Ralph," hissed Henry.
"Shut up," mumbled Ralph rudely.

"I'm . . ." But what could Horrid
Henry say? If he told Ralph he was
– Horrid Henry could barely even
think the word – scared, he'd never
hear the end of it.

Everyone would call him, Henry, leader of the Purple Hand Gang, a goochy goochy nappy baby.
Yikes.

Chapter 4

Should he stay in bed and get eaten by the alien acid monster, or get out of bed and get eaten by the wailing graveyard ghost?

Actually, thought Horrid Henry, the acid monster would get Ralph first, since he was asleep on the floor. But if he jumped really fast, he could race out the door and down the hall to Mum and Dad's room before the graveyard ghost could grab him.

But should he leave Ralph alone
to face the monsters?
Yes! thought Horrid Henry, leaping
out of bed and trampling on Rude
Ralph's head.

"Uhhh," groaned Ralph. "Watch where you're going, you big fat . . ." But Horrid Henry wasn't listening.

He stampeded to the bedroom door,
dashed into the dark hallway and
slammed the door behind him.
Right now he was so scared he didn't
care if he was too old
to jump into Mum and Dad's bed.

Phew. Horrid Henry paused, gasping for breath.

He was safe. The monsters would be too busy chomping on Ralph to nab him.

But wait. Could the graveyard ghost ooze under the door and grab him in the hall? Worse, was the injection bunny gliding up the stairs?

Horrid Henry froze. Oh no.
His heart was pounding.
He opened his mouth to shriek
"MUM!"

Then he closed it.
Wait a minute. Wait a minute.
Peter was sure to be awake,
after all the horrible scary
stories he'd heard today.

After all, Peter was the biggest
scaredy-cat ever. If Henry was scared,
Peter would be a dripping wreck.

He'd just drop in. Seeing Peter
terrified would make him
feel a whole lot better, and
a whole lot braver.
I'll bet Peter's lying there shaking and
too scared to move, thought Horrid
Henry. Ha. Ha. Ha.

Chapter 5

Horrid Henry crept into Peter's room
and shut the door. Then he tip-toed
over to Peter's bed . . .
Huh?

There was Peter, sound asleep, a sweet smile on his face, his peaceful face lit up by his bunny nightlight and ceiling stars.

Horrid Henry's jaw dropped. How could Peter not be having horrible nightmares too?

It was so unfair! He was the brave one, scared of nothing (except injections) and Peter was the wormy worm wibble pants noodle-head who was scared of Rudy the Rootin-Tootin Rooster cartoon, Santa Claus, and probably the Tooth Fairy.

Well, he'd do something
about that.
"Slimy acid monster," murmured
Henry in Peter's ear. "Coming to
get you with his great big googly
eyes and great big monster teeth.

Be afraid, Peter. Be very afraid.
OOOOOOOOOOOHHH."
Perfect Peter smiled in his sleep.
"Hello Mr Monster," he said.

"BOO!" said Horrid Henry.
"BOOO!"
"Would you like a cup of tea?"
murmured Peter.
"No," growled Horrid Henry. "I want
to eat YOU!"

"Okay," said Peter drowsily.
What was wrong with him? thought
Horrid Henry.
"Mwaahahahahahaha," cackled
Horrid Henry. "I'm the graveyard
ghost come to GET ya."

"That's nice," murmured Peter.
"No, it's not nice," growled
Horrid Henry.

"It's scary. It's terrible. Wooooooooooo!
Arrrrggghhhhh! BOOOOOO-
OOOOO-OOO!"
Suddenly Peter's door opened.

Chapter 6

"AAAAAAAARRRRGGGHHH!"
screamed Horrid Henry.
"AAAAAAAARRRRGGGHHH!"
screamed Perfect Peter.
"What are you doing in here,
Henry?" said Mum.

"It's 3 o'clock in the morning,"
said Dad.
Horrid Henry was never so happy to
see anyone in his life.

"I thought Peter would be scared, so I came in to check on him," said Horrid Henry.
Mum stared at Henry.

"And why did you think Peter would be scared?" asked Mum. She looked suspiciously at Henry.

"'Cause I just did," said Henry.

"Go back to your room, Henry," said Mum.

His room? His haunted horrible room where all the monsters were lurking?

"Mum, could you just come with me?" said Henry. "I need you to check on something."

"Can't it wait till morning?" said Dad, yawning.

"No," said Horrid Henry. "I think there's a tarantula under my bed. Could you check please?"
After all, if Mum saw an acid alien there instead of a tarantula, she'd probably mention it.

Mum sighed, walked him to his room
and checked under the bed.
"There's nothing there," said Mum.

"Oh, and in my wardrobe, I'm sure
I saw a . . . umm . . . mouse run in,"
said Henry. "That's what woke me.
Could you just check for me?"
Mum looked in the wardrobe.
"That's it, Henry," snapped Mum.

"Now go to sleep."
Horrid Henry climbed back into bed
and sighed happily. His room looked
just as friendly and familiar as usual.
Why on earth had he been scared?

"Pssst, Ralph, you awake?"
hissed Henry.
"Yeah," said Rude Ralph, sitting up.
"Wanna hear a scary story?" said
Henry. "I know a great one about
a mouldering monster and a cursed
monkey paw . . ."
"Yeah!" said Rude Ralph.

Discover more Horrid Henry Early Readers: